ROTHERHAM LIBRARY AND INFORMATION SERVICES

This book must be returned by the date specified at the time of issue as the DATE DUE for RETURN.

The loan may be extended (personally, by post or telephone) for a further period, if the book is not required by another reader, by quoting the above number/author/title.

LIS 7a

Sshh!

For Merrily and Sophie

Also by Tony Kenyon
Oops! says Olly Bear
No! says Olly Bear

First published in Great Britain in 2002
by Orion Children's Books
This paperback edition published in 2003
by Dolphin Paperbacks
a division of the Orion Publishing Group Ltd
Orion House
5 Upper St Martin's Lane
London   WC2H 9EA

A catalogue record for this book is available from the British Library
Printed and bound in Italy by Printer Trento S.r.l.

ISBN 1 84255 212 0

Hello!
says Olly Bear

TONY KENYON

Dolphin

Olly Bear had a new baby sister.

"Come and give the baby
a hug," said Olly's mum.

"I'm hugging Teddy,"
said Olly.

"Would you like to give the baby her bottle?" asked Olly's dad.

"I'm drinking my juice," said Olly.

"The baby needs her back patting," said Mum.

"Mum," said Olly, "look at my tower."

"Help me bath the
baby," said Dad.

"Can I sail my boat in the water?"
Olly asked.

"There!" said Mum.
"The baby's ready for bed!"

Olly didn't answer.
He was busy with his boat.

Dad put the baby in her cot,

and he and Mum sat
down for a rest.

Olly went on playing.

The baby started crying.

"Mum! Dad! She's making
a noise!" said Olly.

But Mum and Dad
had dozed off.

The baby went on crying . . .

and crying . . .

and crying.

Olly got up
and went to look
in the cot.

The baby stopped crying.

"Hello," said Olly

and the baby smiled and smiled.

But not for long . . .